By Kate Mason

CONTENTS

INTRODUCTION

Cat's Cradle has been a favorite string game for kids for centuries. All you need to weave the figures is a loop of string and a friend. We've included two 6-foot (3.6-m) lengths of string – one for you and one for a friend!

We can only guess when this game was first played and where it came from. Some say it started in Asia, and then caught on in Europe. Charles Lamb, an English writer, wrote about how he and his school friends weaved "cat's cradles" back in 1782!

Weaving string figures was once considered a form of art. Storytellers would wind a loop of string into different figures to act out a story. You can do the same thing with *Cat's Cradle Fun*.

There are Xs and straight strings in most of the figures. Players take turns holding the string figure, while your partner picks up the Xs and winds them over, under, or in between the straight strings. You could make up a story as you go along!

A game of Cat's Cradle has no real end. You can stop at several different figures. It's up to you! Just remember to hold your strings tightly until your partner lets go completely.

Cat's Cradle is easy to learn and fun to share. Keep your loop of string handy. With practice, you can come up with your own new figures!

FIRST THINGS FIRST

The steps in Cat's Cradle use different fingers at different times. Some people use different names for some fingers. Here's how we identify the fingers in the instructions. We'll also show which player's turn it is throughout the book.

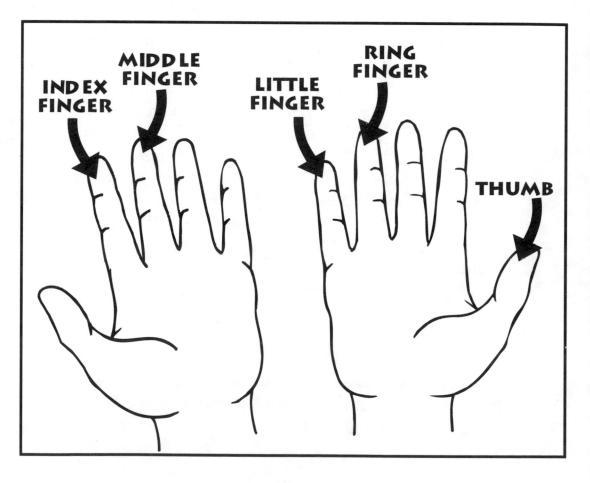

INDEX FINGER

MIDDLE FINGER

LITTLE FINGER

RING FINGER

THUMB

KNOTTING THE STRING

The first thing you need to begin playing Cat's Cradle is a loop of string that won't untie. A square knot works the best. We've included two pieces of string. Use one piece and follow the steps below to make your loop. The second piece of string is extra.

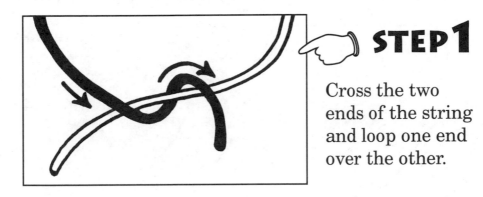

STEP 1

Cross the two ends of the string and loop one end over the other.

STEP 2

Pull the looped end around and up through the center of the knot.

STEP 3

Pull both ends tightly. If the ends are too long, trim them with a scissors.

THE CRADLE

STEP 1

Hold the loop of string around the back of your hands. Leave your thumbs out.

STEP 2

Rotate your hands outward, grabbing the outside string. Bring your hands underneath the outside string to create two inner loops. Your palms should be facing each other.

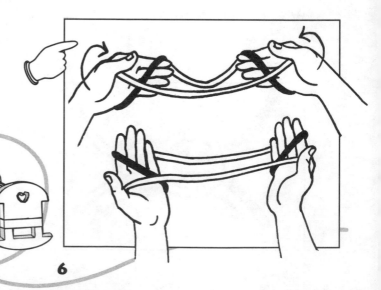

6

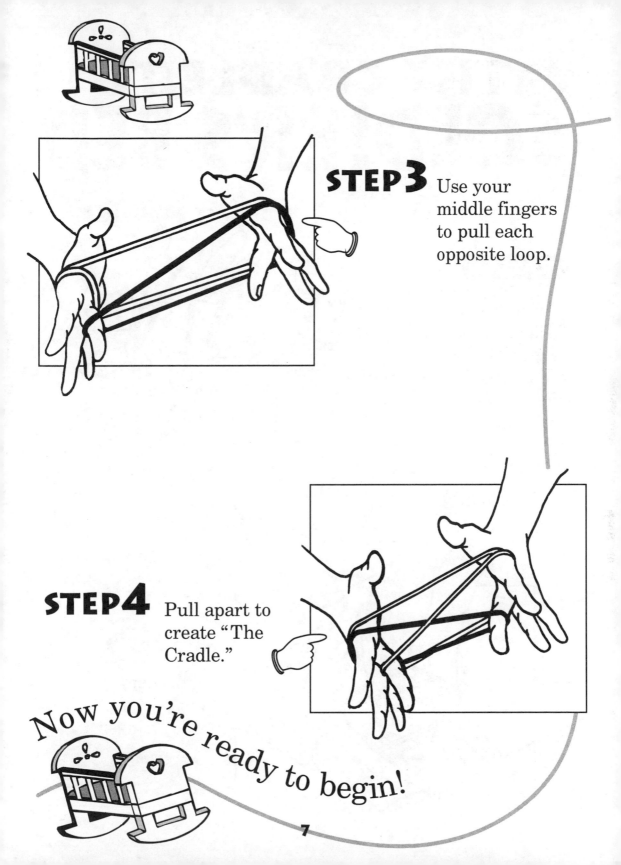

STEP 3
Use your middle fingers to pull each opposite loop.

STEP 4
Pull apart to create "The Cradle."

Now you're ready to begin!

THE CRADLE TO SOLDIER'S BED

PLAYER 2

STEP 1

Use your index fingers and thumbs to grab the two Xs in the figure. Put each thumb on one side of the X and each index finger on the other side, so that the two strings cross between these two fingers.

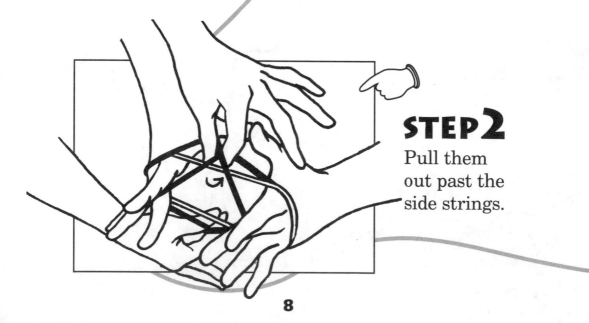

STEP 2

Pull them out past the side strings.

8

Push them
around and
under the side
strings. Turn
your index
fingers up and
through the
center.

STEP 3

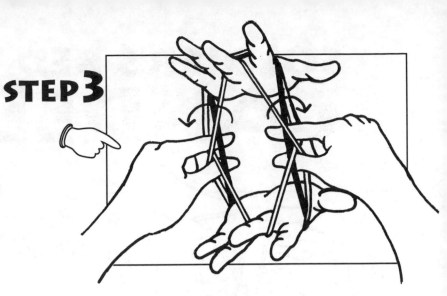

STEP 4 Separate your
thumbs and
index fingers,
and pull tightly.

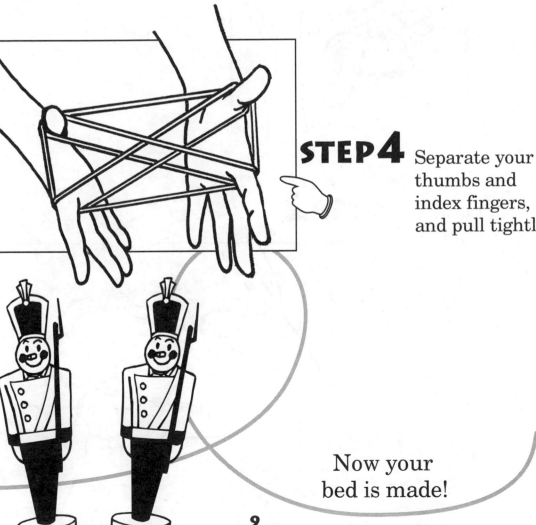

Now your
bed is made!

SOLDIER'S BED TO CANDLES

STEP 1

Grab the Xs with your index fingers and thumbs.

STEP 2

Pull the Xs up and out to the sides.

10

STEP 3

Push the Xs down and under the two side strings. Turn your index fingers and thumbs up and push up and through the center.

STEP 4

Separate your index fingers and thumbs, and pull tightly.

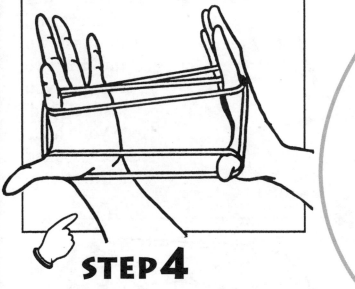

Do you see the candles?

CANDLES TO MANGER

STEP 1

Use your little fingers like hooks to grab the opposite middle strings. Pull them out to the sides.

STEP 2

Push your index fingers and thumbs down into the two triangles you just created. Keep your little fingers hooked to the string!

STEP 3

Push your index fingers and thumbs under the side strings and up through the center. Pull your index fingers and thumbs apart.

MANGER TO DIAMONDS

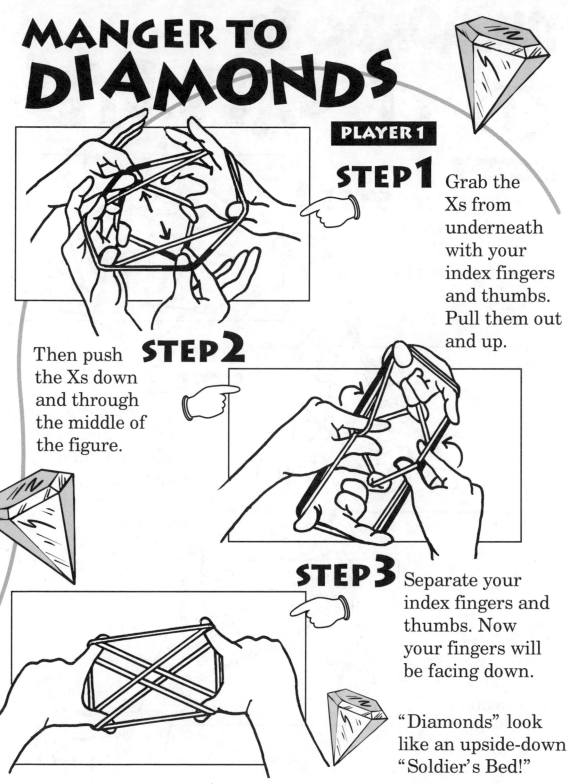

STEP 1

Grab the Xs from underneath with your index fingers and thumbs. Pull them out and up.

STEP 2

Then push the Xs down and through the middle of the figure.

STEP 3

Separate your index fingers and thumbs. Now your fingers will be facing down.

"Diamonds" look like an upside-down "Soldier's Bed!"

13

DIAMONDS TO CAT'S EYES

STEP 1

Grab the Xs with your index fingers and thumbs. Pull them up and out to the sides.

STEP 2

Then push the Xs down and under the side strings. Bring them up through the center.

STEP 3

Turn your index fingers and thumbs up. Now separate them.

CAT'S EYES TO FISH IN A DISH

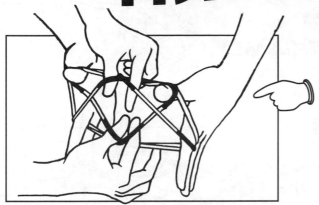

STEP 1

Grab the twisted Xs on the sides with your index fingers and thumbs. Turn your index fingers and thumbs up, making a big diamond in the center.

STEP 2

Separate your index fingers and thumbs.

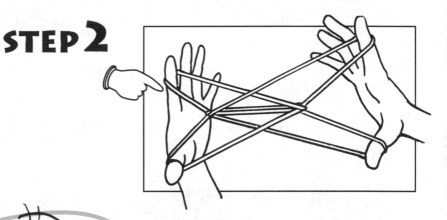

The next move, "Two Royal Crowns," ends the game. If you want to keep playing, skip ahead to "Hand Drum" on page 17. Or, for a surprise, skip ahead to page 23.

FISH IN A DISH TO TWO ROYAL CROWNS
(ENDS THE GAME)

PLAYER 2

STEP 1

Grab the big Xs with your index fingers and thumbs. Pull them up and out. Then push the Xs down and under the side strings. Bring them up through the middle.

STEP 2 Separate your index fingers and thumbs and pull tightly. This move creates the Crowns and ends the game.

Some Cat's Cradle players call this figure the "Grandfather Clock."

16

FISH IN A DISH TO HAND DRUM

(ANOTHER WAY TO END THE GAME)

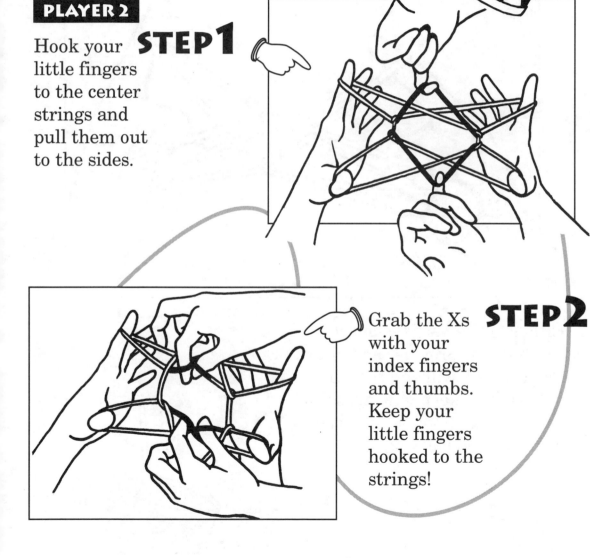

PLAYER 2

STEP 1

Hook your little fingers to the center strings and pull them out to the sides.

STEP 2

Grab the Xs with your index fingers and thumbs. Keep your little fingers hooked to the strings!

Turn your index **STEP 3**
fingers and thumbs up.

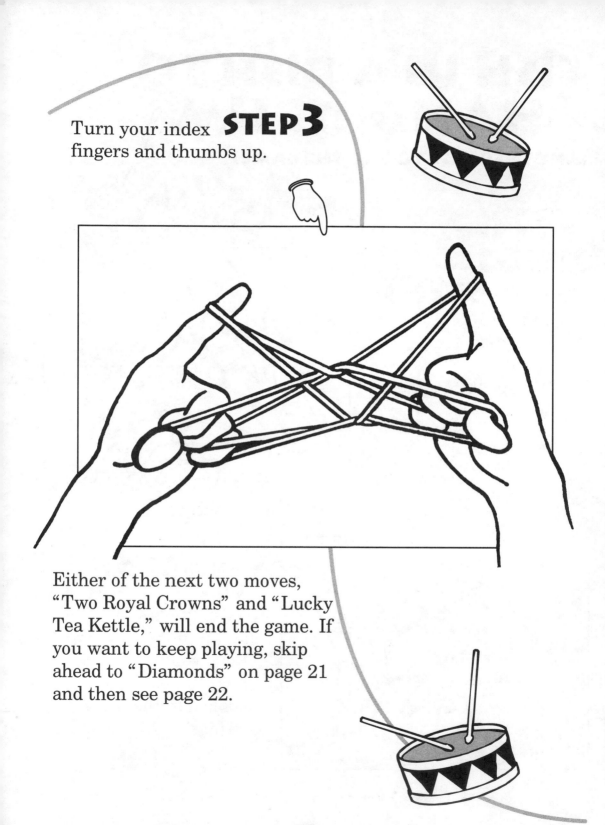

Either of the next two moves,
"Two Royal Crowns" and "Lucky
Tea Kettle," will end the game. If
you want to keep playing, skip
ahead to "Diamonds" on page 21
and then see page 22.

HAND DRUM TO TWO ROYAL CROWNS

(ENDS THE GAME)

PLAYER 2

STEP 1 Unhook the strings from your little fingers.

STEP 2

Pull your hands apart to create "Two Royal Crowns."

This move ends the game. If you have a third player, you can end the game with "Lucky Tea Kettle" on page 20.

HAND DRUM TO LUCKY TEA KETTLE

(ENDS THE GAME)

You will need a third player for this figure.

PLAYER 1

STEP 1

Using your thumb and index finger, grab the loops on Player 2's left thumb and little finger.

PLAYER 3

STEP 2

Using your thumb and index finger, grab the loops from Player 2's right thumb and little finger. Pull tightly.

This is how they end the game in Japan. The Japanese called this figure "the stove" that made the tea kettle boil.

HAND DRUM TO DIAMONDS

(ENDS THE GAME)

STEP 1

With your thumbs and index fingers, grab the two Xs held by Player 2's little fingers. You may have to look for them first. Pull them out to the sides.

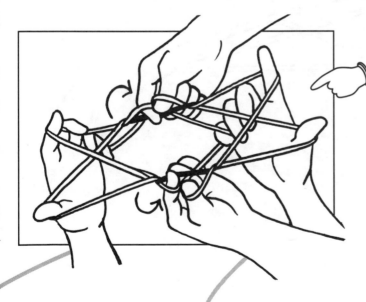

STEP 2

Carefully bring the Xs over the straight string, and then turn your thumbs and index fingers down through the middle of the figure. Separate your fingers to make the "Diamonds." Pull tightly.

Usually this is the end of *Cat's Cradle Fun...*

You could start over, or...

21

KEEP GOING

Once you get to the "Diamonds" again, you can go back to page 14 and turn the "Diamonds" into the "Cat's Eyes." What happens if you keep going from there? It's time to experiment! You may come up with a great new string figure of your own. You can even give it a name!

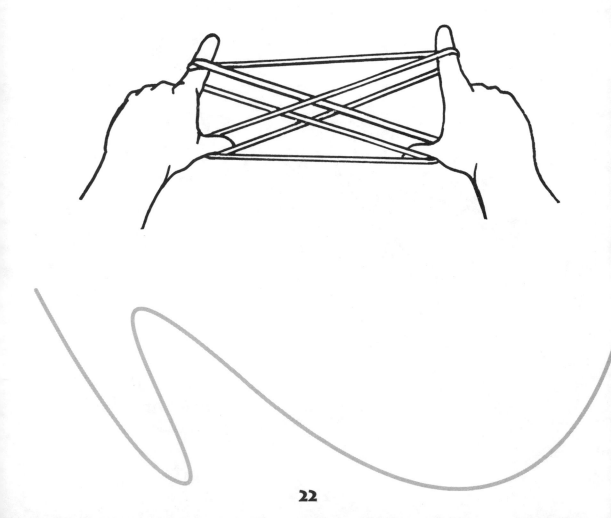

FISH IN A DISH TO ?

For a Cat's Cradle Surprise, start at the beginning. This time stop when you get to "Fish in a Dish" on page 15. Then...

PLAYER 2

STEP 1

With your thumbs and index fingers, grab the two Xs and push down through the center of the figure between the two straight strings. Pull tightly.

What figure did you get? For the answer, turn to the next page...

CAT'S CRADLE SURPRISE

If you came up with "Diamonds," you were correct. You can continue on page 14 to "Cat's Eyes."

Once you've learned all the figures, they will come quickly and naturally to you. The string will feel comfortable on your fingers, and the shapes will start to make sense. You'll see how one figure turns into the next. Then you'll be ready to pass on what you've learned to a friend. That's how the traditional string figures of Cat's Cradle have lasted for so long, and have traveled all over the world.